My Daddy and I

Also by P. K. Hallinan

P. K. Hallinan

My Daddy and I

ideals children's books®

Nashville, Tennessee

ISBN 0-8249-5521-8

Published by Ideals Children's Books
An imprint of Ideals Publications
A division of Guideposts
535 Metroplex Drive, Suite 250
Nashville, Tennessee 37211
www.idealsbooks.com

Copyright © 2005 by P. K. Hallinan

Printed and bound in Italy by LEGO

Library of Congress CIP data on file

Designed by Georgina Chidlow-Rucker

10 9 8 7 6 5 4 3 2 1

With special thanks
to dads everywhere

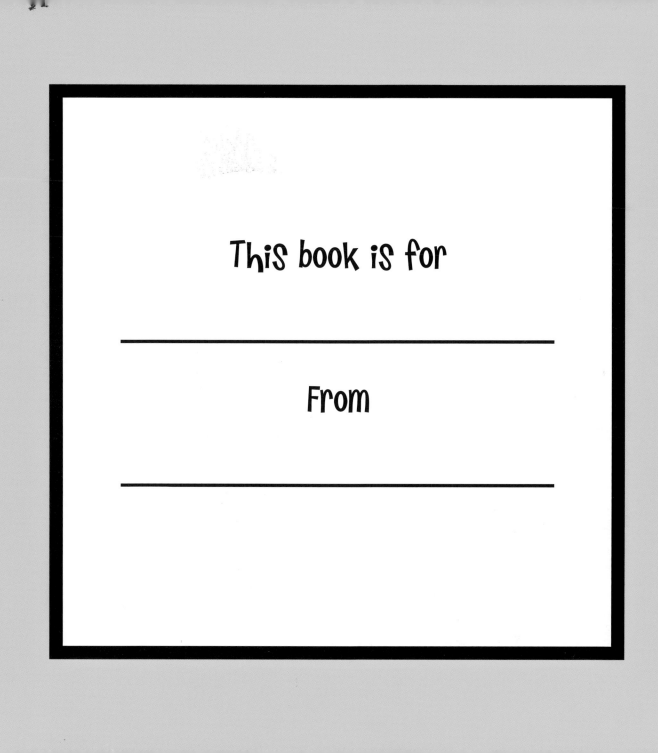

This book is for

_____

From

We're very good friends,
My daddy and I.

We like to play catch

And watch trains roar by.

And sometimes we'll sit
At the base of a tree
And talk about places
We wish we could see.

Or sometimes we'll walk,
And we won't say a word.
But that's okay too
For good friends to do.

We like to play sports,
My daddy and I,

Like tennis

And horseshoes

And fishing with flies.

In winter we'll go
For a romp in the snow!

In summer we'll play
At the beach the whole day!

But then there are times
That we just sit and stare
At far-distant stars
That light the night air.

We really like stars,
My daddy and I.

And always we're happy
Just being together,
Like clams in the sand
Or birds of a feather.

And we like to play cards.

We even like mowing
And hoeing the yard.

But once in a while,
We'll just take a drive
And feel all the gladness
Of being alive.

We always have fun,
My daddy and I.

Then, in the evening,
We usually stand
Alone in the kitchen
And talk man-to-man.

And I see in his eyes
How deeply he cares,
And I hear in his voice
All the feelings he bears.

My daddy's my teacher.

He's my leader, my guide.

And I like being with him,
Right there at his side.

He's helped me to grow
And to stand very tall.

And I know in my heart
He's the best dad of all!

So I guess, in the end,
Love's the best reason why . . .

We're very good friends,
My daddy and I.